NICKELODEON

iCarly

iHatch Chicks!

by Victoria Kosara

D0972399

SCHOLASTIC INC.

New York   Toronto   London   Auckland

Sydney   Mexico City   New Delhi   Hong Kong

ISBN: 978-0-545-20128-5

Published by Scholastic Inc.
SCHOLASTIC and associated logos are trademarks and/or registered trademarks of Scholastic Inc.

12 11 10 9 8 7 6 5 4 3 2 1   10 11 12 13 14 15/0

Designed by Angela Jun
Printed in the U.S.A.   40
First printing, January 2010

Carly Shay and her best friend, Samantha Puckett, walked to their lockers after science class. They were going to be partners for their science project.

Carly's neighbor, Freddie Benson, joined them. He was upset because his partner for the project was Duke. Duke was a crazy wrestler.

Right then, Duke walked over to them. "Hey, what's up, Fray-doe?" Duke yelled. He tried a wrestling move on Freddie.

Carly helped Freddie free himself from Duke's hold. Then, the boys talked about their science project. They needed to pick something to study.

"Why don't we do a study on why my kneepads stink so bad?" Duke shouted. He shoved his smelly kneepad in Freddie's face.

It wasn't going to be an easy project.

Carly and Sam went to Carly's loft after school. Carly's older brother, Spencer, was in the kitchen.

"Hey, what are you ladies up to?" asked Spencer.

"We're just trying to pick a topic for our science project," Carly answered.

Spencer looked at the carton of eggs in the fridge. He took one out and held it up. "When I was in school, we hatched a bunch of baby chicks in the classroom. Very cool, very fun!" he said.

Carly and Sam thought it was a great idea for a science project. Spencer said they could hatch the chicks in the apartment.

Carly, Sam, and Freddie had a Web show called *iCarly*. The girls couldn't wait to share their project on their next Webcast.

"Hey, it's time for *iCarly*!" Sam said.
Freddie was filming Sam and Carly for
iCarly. They were in their studio at Carly's
loft. The theme of the show was eggs. The
girls explained to the viewers that they were
hatching chicks for their school science project.

There were six eggs. Sam and Carly had named them Shelly, Huevo, Omelet, Benedict, Yoko, and Poachy. The eggs would sit in a special heated box called an incubator until they hatched. Then the chicks had to stay in there until they were old enough to live outside.

Freddie had set up a camera to watch the eggs. He called it the Egg-Cam. *iCarly* viewers could watch the Egg-Cam on the *iCarly* Website.

A few days later, Spencer came out from the bathroom holding the chick named Shelly. Carly and Sam were surprised.

"Our chicks haven't hatched yet!" said Carly.

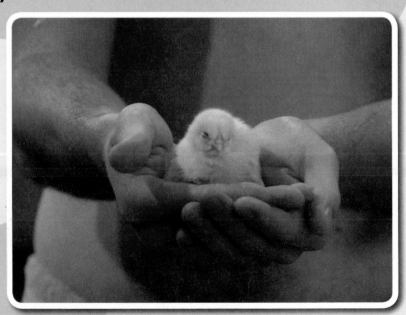

"Have they?" Sam and Carly screamed, and ran upstairs to check the incubator.

"They all hatched!" Sam said when they got there. There were only empty eggshells in the incubator. The girls were worried. The chicks were too young to be out of the incubator. They could be anywhere in the whole apartment! Carly and Sam had to find the chicks fast.

Just then Freddie came over. He had seen the chicks hatch on the Egg-Cam. But he didn't know that all the chicks were missing.

"They escaped!" Carly told Freddie. The three friends decided to go online. They needed to find out how long baby chicks could live outside the incubator.

They found a Website called "Chickapedia."
It said that baby chicks needed to live in
the incubator until they were one week old.
They also needed to be fed every four
hours.

Using the Egg-Cam, Freddie figured
out that the chicks had escaped fifty-six
minutes ago. That meant that they had three
hours and four minutes to find the other five
chicks.

"Okay. We can do this, right?" asked Carly.
"Yes! Absolutely!" said Freddie and Sam.
They all ran downstairs to start the search for the chicks.

Spencer turned the heat up to ninety degrees. That way the loft was as hot as the incubator.

Carly put up a big board next to the incubator. The board had the pictures and names of all the chicks on it. Spencer put a big check mark next to Shelly because they had already found her.

Carly, Sam, Freddie, and Spencer each took a walkie-talkie. Then they split up to look for the chicks.

Carly ran into the kitchen. She heard peeping right away. It was coming from the sink! She listened closely.

"He's stuck in the pipe down there!" she said.

Carly carefully unscrewed the pipe with a wrench. But she could not fit her hand inside the pipe to grab the chick. Luckily, Sam knew just what to do.

"Cup your hands under the pipe," Sam told her. Sam blew into the pipe as hard as she could. The chick popped out and landed safely in Carly's hands.

"Four to go!" yelled Carly. "Keep looking upstairs," she said to Sam.

Carly placed the chick back in the incubator. Then she put a big red check next to Huevo.

Peep, peep, peep.
"I think I hear one in this heating duct,"
Spencer said.

Spencer crawled into the vent to catch the baby chick. "I see him!" he yelled. But Spencer was too big for the heating duct. When Spencer reached for the chick, he discovered he was stuck.

"Will you guys pull me out of here?" Spencer asked.

Duke had just come over to work with Freddie on their project. Duke, Freddie, Carly, and Sam pulled and pulled. But they could not get Spencer out of the vent. Finally, Spencer told them to find the chicks first. Then they could come back to pull him out.

Freddie and Duke looked in the kitchen.
Peep, peep.

"Hey, I think I hear one behind the fridge!" said Freddie.

"Back up. I'll move the fridge," Duke told him.

Duke tried and tried to pick it up, but the fridge was very heavy. Finally, he lifted it.

Freddie ran to the chick. "Got him!" he said.

Freddie put Omelet back in the incubator with Huevo and Shelly, and placed a check mark next to Omelet's name on the board.

Then Duke heard another peep in the living room. It was coming from the wall. Duke smashed a hole in the wall with his head! Maybe having Duke as a partner wasn't so bad after all! Freddie reached into the wall and pulled out chick number four. It was Benedict! They put him back with the other chicks, and checked off his name.

Meanwhile, Carly and Sam were upstairs in the *iCarly* studio.

"There's another chick on that beam," said Sam. She helped Carly climb up to the beam. "Be careful!" Sam said to Carly.

Carly tried to grab the chick. But she accidentally knocked him off the beam! Sam dove onto the floor. She caught the chick just in time.

There was only one chick left to find!

"We found Yoko!" Carly said, running downstairs. She placed Yoko back in the incubator. Sam put a check next to Yoko's name.

"Okay, we've found Shelly, Huevo, Omelet, Benedict, and Yoko," said Sam.

"Now we've just got to find Poachy!" Carly said.

They only had nine minutes left to find Poachy. Then all of the chicks needed to eat. Sam and Carly ran to search upstairs. Freddie started looking downstairs. Duke had left to get a smoothie. Spencer was still stuck in the heating duct.

Everyone was worried that they would not find Poachy in time. Just then, they heard peeping. It was Poachy! He was stuck in the elevator shaft behind a window. Carly and Sam tried to pull the frame off the window. The frame was stuck!

Carly called Freddie on her walkie-talkie.

"Freddie! We found the last chick. We need tools to get to him!" she said.

Freddie pushed the elevator button to come upstairs to help.

"No, no! Don't use the elevator!" Carly yelled. But it was too late. The doors closed.

The girls ran downstairs to see if Poachy was still in the elevator. But when the doors opened, he was not there.

"He was in the elevator shaft. He could be anywhere in the whole building by now," Carly said sadly.

Carly checked the time. It had been longer than three hours and four minutes. It was too late to save Poachy. Sam, Carly, and Freddie were very sad.

Then they heard Spencer making a weird noise in the vent.

"Let's try to pull him out of there again!" said Freddie.

"One, two, three!" Carly counted.

They pulled hard. Finally, Spencer was free! But it looked like he had something in his mouth.

"Are you all right?" Sam asked.

Spencer coughed. He opened his mouth and spit a chick out into his hand. It was Poachy! "You saved him!" Carly shouted.

"Yeah, but he didn't even taste like chicken!" Spencer said.

Carly smiled.

She put Poachy back in the incubator with the other five chicks. Together they had saved all six of the chicks!